The Horn of Life

Flying Worlds Science Fiction Short Story

Newsletter

Sign Up to my Newsletter.

- Learn first about new Releases.

- Read exclusive background information.

- Get special fan extras.

Sign up here:

Or here:
https://blog.topazhauyn.com/newsletter/

for me

The Horn of Life
Flying Worlds Science Fiction Short Story

TOPAZ HAUYN

Morag Merrim held the brown, bent wood in the diameter of her arm in his shaking hands. The Horn of Life, that was important for survival on the Flora.

Whereas this place wasn't the energy room. Neither was it anything he ever saw on the spaceship in his life.

Half an hour earlier Morag had come on duty. He had finished the few reports waiting on his desk for approval. He was proud of always having a clean desk. Or clean enough to see part of the floral ornament engraved in the tabletop by an unknown ancestor.

He liked his work as head of the energy bubbly team. Being responsible for four people and the whole source of energy at the spaceship was an important job. And he did everything in his powers to make the flow of energy coming from the energy room stable and constant. Always up to the need of the spaceship and all inhabitants, which were many.

The downside of his job, if anyone ever bothered to ask, was that he had so little time left doing the real work: Tending the energy bubbles, caring for them. Most of the time he sat in discussions about enhancement projects. The Flora had become too small for all people living on it. A new addition should be attached to it.

Obviously this needed lots of energy to craft it, but also more energy to operate it later.

The first wasn't that much of a discussion. He had enough auxiliary energy bubbles to deal with sudden spikes.

The latter, a constantly higher need was a whole other topic.

When Benedikt Mil had called in sick, Morag had decided not to put Annabell in the place, but to use the chance and tend the energy bubbles himself for a change.

Happy he had stepped through the ID guarded door into the energy room.

The gray shelves filling the huge room from one side to the other, only left a rectangular space at the door and the opposite end free. Enough to place a few hanging cupboards with special white gloves for the work.

Next to them in another open cupboard hung the Horn of Life. The brown, bend wood, in diameter of his arm.

He never understood how it worked, but it did.

If one brushed the Horn over an energy bubble, it brightened. The augmentation in energy could be measured. But the augmentation fell over time back and under the original energy state.

Morag had hummed a lullaby he has sung for his two-year-old son every evening. He put on a pair of white special gloves and picked the Horn of Life. To him, it looked more like a thicker stick, randomly picked up with its furrowed bark, from its cupboard.

Aisle DA shelve T was due today, according to the foster plan.

The steps of his boots on the floor had echoed down the aisle. The ladder to climb up to shelve T had been already in place.

Morag remembered that as odd, because tools were returned to their place after work. Which in the case of the ladder meant, at the far end of the aisle.

He had climbed up and tended the first few worlds, glowing bright red and green afterwards, when he heard steps in the energy room.

He had climbed back down to take a look.

Richard Henry, one of his team, stood in the door, smiling at him.

"Hi, boss", said Richard Henry. "Benedikt called me. Told me to take his shift."

"No need. Thank you for coming. I already took over", said Morag and waved Richard Henry out. "You stay with the next shift as planned."

Without a second glance he had turned and walked back to the ladder.

He wasn't going to let this opportunity go now. And after all, he made the staff roster and could plan replacements. He liked Benedikt Mill, a competent worker, but today he wanted to do the hands-on himself.

»You sure I can't help?«, asked Richard Henry's voice below him from the ground.

»Can you check the other ladders? That one hadn't been on its regular spot«, said Morag.

He looked at the yellow world in front of him, brushed the bent stick around it. The yellow became a bright yellow, nearly blinding his sight for a moment. It was amazing how much influence this piece of wood had over the energy bubbles.

Which reminded him of the second thing in his career he hadn't achieved: Creating an energy bubble himself. Sadly the bubble creator was the only person to achieve that, and he hadn't been chosen.

Morag climbed down and moved the ladder down the shelf to reach the next world. In the distance he heard the echoes of Richard Henry's steps, as he walked the aisles, checking for ladders not at their place.

He tended a red world, when his ladder rocked.

He grabbed the board of the shelf to steady himself with his free hand. "What the?", Morag exclaimed.

Looking down, Morag saw Richard Henry holding the sides of his ladder.

"Let go", ordered Morag. "What do you think you are doing with that ladder?"

Richard Henry shrugged and grinned like he enjoyed himself. "Returning the ladder to its place, as instructed."

"Idiot!", growled Morag under his breath, low enough the man at the floor wouldn't hear him, for there were twenty shelves between them, at least two times his own height.

»Don't think so«, called Richard Henry back. "I always finish my tasks."

And he pulled at the ladder hard enough to let it wobble.

Morag nearly let go the Horn of Life in his hand.
Nearly.
He grabbed tight around it in the last instant, locked his feet around a round rung of the ladder. His free hand

hadn't managed to hold on to the board of the shelf and hit the red energy bubble next to him.

He felt heat flare against his hand. Pulled his hand back, fighting for his balance even more.

Morag glanced at his glove. The palm was black and got a hole.

A hole?

That shouldn't happen to the special gloves. They needed to be checked if they had thinned after generations using them.

"I have another task for you to do first." Morag shouted to drown out the clattering of the ladder against the shelf and his own uniform clothes rustling from his rapid movements.

"Yes?", asked the deep voice of Richard Henry from the floor. "But only if you first release me from that task and", he shook the ladder again, sending Morag in a new round of fighting for balance, "promise that task never shows up as not completed in my work record. I have a work ethic to lose!"

"Sure. Never will", promised Morag.

Richard Henry acted odd.

He would remove him from the team as soon as he got down from the ladder and out to his desk in the office in front of the energy room. Work ethic, what a joke. Richard Henry called sick more often than not.

To Morag, that was no work ethic, no matter the fact, the man really finished all tasks given to him.

The question was always: Were the results the desired and expected ones?

"Go, check the gloves for holes. This one is busted."

At least, Richard Henry stopped jerking the ladder. Morag pulled the glove off his hand, using his teeth. The fabric was sturdy, and he had to try several times to grab it properly with his teeth.

He smelled the smoke of burned material coming from the palm without the glove. It tasted like licking on stewed metal. Nothing he'd ever volunteer to try again.

When he got the glove off, he threw it down. With a low thud it landed next to Richard Henry.

"Bring me a new one, please. The first whole one you find", said Morag.

He watched how the other man fetched the broken glove and stomped down the aisle towards the front.

Relived with the outcome Morag checked his bare hand: Unmarred. The glove had kept the fire.

He moved the Horn of Life from his hand with the glove into his bare hand. It wouldn't hurt to continue working as long as the hand holding the energy bubbles was protected, he decided. The Horn of Life had no real contact with the energy bubbles, thus, there was no danger in fostering the rest of them.

Only two more to go on this shelve before he had to move the ladder again. By then, his new glove would be surely brought to him. No need to climb the height of twenty shelves twice.

The next bubble in row was a blue one. This one glowed faintly. Its shine flickered and already got some hints of green at its tips. It wouldn't last much longer if not cared.

The problem with the change of color was the level of energy the worlds provided in the future. The blue ones where the best energy sources. Sadly the Horn of Life could only augment the energy bubbles. It couldn't raise them up in the level of energy to the next higher color.

Morag remembered the last time he had tried it with a red world, which was short of falling apart at the end of her life. When he augmented and augmented it even more, at one point the red world imploded. Now, as a reminder for him and everyone after him, it sat on its place as a little black dot. Or more accurate, it hovered over its place.

Morag held the brown wood at the perfect distance to the blue world, watching the green tips vanish from the shine.

The blue world was saved for now.

The ladder jerked again.

"Stop it you idiot!", shouted Morag without looking down. He had to make do, finding his balance once more. He put the Horn of Life on the shelf to hold on the ladder and shelve, avoiding to fall.

»What's wrong with you? Do you want to kill me?«

"Sure", answered Richard Henry with a dry voice. »If you're gone, I'll be promoted.«

Cold fear knotted into Morag's belly. Richard Henry really was crazy.

"Well. I can tell the Zora you earned a promotion", Morag suggested and started to climb down the ladder. "Wait a minute and we can talk."

»No. We can't talk. I get your place and will never again be called an idiot by you!«, shouted Richard Henry. He jerked the ladder even more.

»Where's the whole glove?«, asked Morag to distract the man rambling on about insulting words and his plans of changing the energy room the moment Morag was gone.

»Back in the cupboard, where it belongs. Sad thing you didn't die touching the red world«, spat Richard Henry.

Morag was already halfway down the ladder, when it dawned on him, that the hole in the glove already was an attack on him.

»I guess, Benedikt Mill isn't sick then?«, Morag asked as calmly as he could.

"No. I asked him to switch and faked the call", admitted Richard Henry. "Clever. You never thought I could to this, right. Yet, I could. I know a lot more than you do", he bragged.

Only four more shelves until the floor, thought Morag. He had to keep the man talking.

But before he could ask another question. The ladder was jerked again. Its side hit the protruding end of the Horn of Life, send it circling into the air.

Morag watched it fall like in slow motion.

It descended from the T shelve, nearly parallel to the jerking ladder. Until it was hit again and started flying sideways towards a world on the other side of the aisle.

Morag let the ladder go. He stretched his hands to catch the Horn of Life. Without it, they wouldn't be able to foster the worlds. Not only the plans for the new addition to the Flora would be jeopardized. The current supply would be too.

He needed to catch it, before it burned from the contact with one of the energy bubbles.

The bend stick brushed painful against his bare hands fingertips.

Morag pushed with his feet against the rung of the ladder, to get a hold of the artifact. His fingers closed around the bend in the middle of the Horn of Life the moment he felt the back of his hand contact something warm.

Out of the corner of his eyes he saw a flash of blue.

He had touched an energy bubble with his bare skin.

Before he could do anything, everything went black. Only the feel about the rough, warm wood in his hand remained.

Then, he had opened his eyes again. Although he wasn't sure if this was the right term, for he never closed it. It felt more like a curtain got lifted from him.

The first thing he had perceived was the air smelling sweet like the skin of his baby son. Then, he saw the rich, deep green hills all around him. Animals walked past them, he didn't recognize.

Wherever he was, he wasn't on the Flora anymore.

THE END

Excerpt: Discovery

The weather in the light green, oval meadow was warm and sunny. If one could call the lightened up ceiling, to imitate an Earth day during summer, sunny.

The ceiling mimicked a blue sky, when in reality, every-thing was black outside of each window build into the outer skin of the spaceship. A thorough black strewn with sparkling stars every now and then. Combined with the vast emptiness of space, being inside, relaxing in this artificial place, this gem of a blue sky, gave Alexandra a faint feel of reality.

A reality like it once had been.

Alexandra von Humboldt knew a lot about making up realities to survive in the parochial space provided by their spaceship, called Flora. No matter the fact, that the Flora got enlarged by generations living here, until it was the size of the former Moon circling the Earth, the sheer sum of people living in it, used up every bit of space.

She leaned against the stone bench behind her in the middle of the meadow. She took in the fresh air, that felt humid and smelled of dry leaves, waiting for rain to come. A vast contrast to the stale air filling all corridors and rooms outside of the gardens. Somehow the air circulation never got the sour, stale air to be as fresh as here, between the plants.

This was her day off of her duties in the energy room. Her birthday.

She was intent on enjoying her day and not thinking of the problems she had at work. Especially with her being lucky on getting the meadow for herself alone for a quarter-hour. Waiting lists were long, and she knew she had been privileged to get this spot, despite becoming only twenty-seven. Later she would meet with Annabell, her co-worker who had promised to bake Alexandra's favorite cake for her.

The birds living in the trees framing the meadow and the little creek rustling along at the northern side livened up the still oasis of nature amidst all the technology. The singing of the birds made Alexandra smile with joy.

Her body relaxed from the fun of just listening to animals.

Living animals. Not recorded sounds of a long gone Earth time. Done with recording equipment that wasn't up to the quality of sound recording she was used to.

A brown bird, with a red throat, flew past Alexandra. The flap of his wing sounding loud in the otherwise muted environment.

She watched him dive into the surface of the creek.

Water splashed. The bird resurfaced, shook and flew around the meadow. Throwing little drops of water all around him on his way. Artificial sunlight broke itself in the drops and produced a glowing rainbow.

Alexandra memorized her observations. This experience and imagery would make for a great world at work.

Work. The thought alone made her drop her smile. She felt frustration rise to her forehead, giving her the feel of a starting headache. Her hands closed into fists.

Her ability of turning her leisure time experiences into new worlds was what got her this exclusive time in the meadow. Not her age. Just the fact, that she, as the current creator of the energy bubbles could form the images into energy bubbles. The fuel keeping the Flora working.

Therefore, she had to quickly get the artifact, the bubble flower, back and return to her work.

The thought of how the bubble flower went missing a few weeks back threatened her position. Without it, she couldn't create more spectacular, energy sources called 'bubbles' by her coworkers.

Alexandra's problem, more major than the missing issue, was that the surveillance records of the energy room listed her as the last one who saw it, touched it.

Alexandra felt the dry grass under her hands. She rubbed a single grass stalk between her fingertips. Slender, hard, with a sharper tip than one would expect from a stalk.

She didn't pull it out. Growing the grass in the meadow was too much a work to just pull one culm out and destroy it.

Alexandra watched the bird with the read throat disappear. As did the sparkling rainbow spanning over the creek. And with it stopped the vivid memory of the mesmerizing color play of the bubble flower.

Could she produce such a rainbow by herself?

She longed to move down to the creek and splash the water. Try it out. The idea felt like this would be fun. Despite knowing perfectly well it was forbidden.

She wanted to do fun things more often, too. Yet, here she sat, filled with worries, at her favorite place on the whole spaceship on the only spare day of the year, her birthday.

Her plan had been to enjoy the garden section. To feel the warm grass and breath the air, refreshed by real trees instead of air cleaner.

Instead of celebrating, or eating healthy snacks, Alexandra forced her thoughts to quit thinking about the energy problems and the missing artifacts. Without the bubble flower they couldn't create new bubbles of energy. Without the horn of life, they couldn't nurture the remaining bubbles.

At least, she wasn't responsible for the whereabouts of the horn of life. That had gone missing together with the bubble creator who had been on the job before her. Which was another story wrapped into unanswered questions. She hadn't even known her predecessor.

Lacking a way to nurture the energy bubbles, they got used up faster. Alexandra had created energy bubble after energy bubble for two years in a row now. Every day. Without pause. Until a few weeks back everything came to a halt. A welcome halt for her. The first time since she got pushed into the job she had time to step back and look at things. The bubble flower got lost. Thanks to the fact that this event gave her a pause, she was suspect to hiding it. Though she had searched with everybody else. The bubble flower still was missing, and she had now way proving she hadn't stolen it.

The energy bubbles were urgently needed to keep the engines working. The energy they delivered, compared to the space they needed, was nearly indefinite. Only now and then a new mind artist with fantasy to create new worlds had been needed. And even then, there was no need for originality, as long as worlds were formed.

But that had changed for her.

Alexandra pulled her knees close and folded her arms around her gray uniform trousers. Even her jacket was gray. Only one golden button was used at the cuffs each. The symbol engraved on the buttons was a flower unlike the earthly flowers grown in this garden during spring. It's twelve petals consisted of little orbs forming triangular pyramid.

History had it, that the moment the bubble flower was manufactured, all energy sources on Earth instantly vanished.

Like poof. They were gone. As was most of the life on Earth that moment. Nobody knew why or how. Only the bubble flower remained. Together with the only finished spaceship to travel the galaxy and search for a new home.

The orbs on the button were yellow like the button

itself.

Alexandra had a painting hung at the door of the little box she sometimes stored her hammock in during the day. On that image, the orbs of the bubble flower shimmered in all the colors of the rainbow. So did the energy bubbles at her work. The ones she was responsible to take care for. Even, when one of the energy bubbles wasn't a useful energy source anymore, it now was fostered by Alexandra and her coworkers as well, for the people living on this spaceship.

They were dependent from them: Energy. Travel. Both things were inseparable tied to the rainbow shimmering orbs.

Even discovering new worlds to live on had a lower priority. Or so her superior Richard Henry always said. Something she doubted, because otherwise she would report to person higher in the hierarchy, wouldn't she?

Probably a reason, why the Flower, as the first crew had named the spaceship, never reached her goal: Finding a perfect new planet for mankind to live on.

How would anybody deem a planet perfect with the work waiting for them to make the planet a new home?

Alexandra heard the deep buzzing sound of the doors sliding open. Her quarter-hour was up. She heard the chatter of voices and the steps of people coming in. People chatting, feet stomping on the grass, the noise quickly approached her in the meadow with the stone bench she comfortably leaned against.

Her solitary time in the meadow was over for this year. With luck, she would be able to come next year.

Alexandra got up and out of the garden.

Walking past the new arrivals she stepped through the gray gate that stood open.

The stale air, always smelling of old metal needing cleaning urgently, pressed in on Alexandra.

She hurried past the queue of people who waited to be allowed into the garden as fast as she could. Which was a slow crawl in reality.

All the people stood near the wall. They tried to make themselves small and let her pass.

She walked sideways to be smaller. Her gray uniform rubbed against the metal wall behind her, adding another sound to the loudness in the aisle. Yet, she hadn't enough space. Most people she slipped past had to press against their side of the aisle to let her pass through.

Most aisles provided more space. But the gardens were part of the oldest part of the Flora where aisles were low and narrow. Compared with the others' curious glances and the obvious thoughts, Alexandra found this walk humiliating. It was pretty visible in the crowds narrowed eyebrows and smirking smiles that everybody knew about her privilege of solitary nature time.

The calm Alexandra had found in the garden evaporated.

Excerpt end of: Discovery

More books

Tahir al Kalim trades with the powers of the universe, with the traders from beyond his world. For others. Always successful. Never for himself.

Today differs. He needs a trade for himself, for his country, his family. The importance hinders his concentration.

With the prince already dead, Tahir only sees one chance to right everything. To right his false customer choice.

A Merchant Universe short story. And an electrifying tale of a man whose concentration will shape the future of his people.

Fantasy

Beaten Path in the Mist
Vampire Hunting with the Tiger Eye
Marlene's New Monster
Remorse of the Mermaid
Wipe off the Dust
The Book Burning
Stars Flying into Philosophy
Red: #890000
The True Mage Survives
The Flower on the Mountain Top
The speaking Mirror

The Fork with the Scales
Fairy Needs Courage
The Rainbow Bubble Collapse
Repair the Music
The missing Jack O'Lantern

Wishing Well World
- A Fairies Wish (#1)
- Fantasy Sweets (#2)
- Hodur at Christmas Eve (#3)

Merchant Universe
- Merchant of all Power (#1)
- Lifa's first trade (#2)

Romance

M/F, Hetero Romantik
World Cup and Pink Ropes
An Invitation to a Wedding
Corrupted Food Storage
Fighting the Cinnamon Guy
Forgotten Communications
The Magic Book
Love against all Rules
Love as a Christmas Present
The Griffin's Wedding Ring
Crossroads with Half the

Information (Collection)
Love over Tomato Soup

Secret Southwest Forest Shifters
- Welcome my Wolf (#1)
- Research my Wolf (#2)
- Love my Wolf (#3)

F/F, Lesbische Romantik
Dance to your Love
Reverse Harem / Ménage
Love the Forbidden Partners

Science Fiction

Abandonned Time Travel
Alien Visit
Coloring an Apple

Corrupted Food Storage
Red: #890000
Served like red Wine

Shards of her Life
Support Refused
Sweet Depths
The Water Theft
Lottery Win: The Third Set of
Doors
Human Interactions Preferred

Intertwined Fate
Theft on the Generation Ship
Flying Worlds
- Dicovery (#1)
- Horn of Life (#2)
- Tika discovers the ocean (#3)

Mystery

Eating Out Adventure
Life Changing Game
The Lady Says: Die
The One Time Chance
Intertwined Fate

If date equals…
Keyring
Who paid for the bullet?
Theft on the Generation Ship

Contemporary

The Curses of Operating
Systems
Firefighter Dressed Wrong
Habits burning in the Solar
Eclipse
Wild Majoram

The Rags of an Orphan
Architecture Impress
An Authors first Success
Postcard from a warmer Place
The Meeting Contact
Company Sold